Disney
Hundred-Acre Adventures
Rainy Day

Ladybird

It was a fine, sunny afternoon, and the sun was shining brightly, as it is supposed to do on sunny afternoons. Pooh and Piglet went to visit Rabbit.

'Good day,' said Pooh as he raised his paw to cover his eyes from the glare of the sun.

'Good day,' said Piglet, lowering his ears to shade his eyes.

'It's not a good day for me,' grumbled Rabbit. 'The ground is so dry nothing will grow!'

Rabbit looked up at the sky. 'Those clouds in the distance… They had better burst into rain before my plants wilt completely,' he said.

'You're right, Rabbit,' Piglet said. 'Your vegetables do need rain, but I like sunny days better than rainy ones,' he sighed.

'*Boing!*'

The friends turned round. They knew this sound very well – and they knew who was making it! Tigger!

'Piglet, you look worried,' Tigger said as he landed.

Piglet blinked. 'Rabbit said the clouds are going to burst and that it's going to storm! It's so loud when it storms!'

Tigger inspected the horizon. 'Storm? I see Pooh, I see Rabbit, I see Piglet… but I don't see any clouds at all!'

5

'Really?' Piglet asked, and looked around himself just to be sure.

'Yes, really!' Tigger said, and bounced around, knocking Pooh and Piglet onto their backs.

This is how Piglet and Pooh came to be lying on their backs, looking at the sky.

And from this angle, they were finally able to see some clouds coming into view.

'As usual, there are those who can lie around whilst others work!' growled Rabbit. He grabbed his watering can and went to get some water. 'If only it would rain, for heaven's sake.

As soon as Rabbit left, a group of tiny white clouds passed above our friends. 'Look carefully, Piglet,' said Pooh. 'Here comes a big sheep right above us!'

'It looks more like a pig to me. Oh, Pooh, look! There is a big pillow running after it!'

Pooh didn't answer. He was counting. The clouds had started to look like honey pots, and they were becoming bigger and rounder!

'I would need another cupboard if I had to store all this honey,' Pooh thought to himself.

'Oh! Oh! Oh!' Tigger cried. 'Here comes a cloud that looks just like Eeyore!'

A grey cloud had appeared and the sunlight made it shimmer nicely.

'But I never saw Eeyore smile like that!' joked Tigger with a hearty laugh.

Suddenly, the shuffle of Eeyore's weary feet could be heard. 'If I were you,' Eeyore sighed, gloomily, 'I wouldn't laugh. Bad weather is coming again.'

'But Tigger said the clouds wouldn't bring rain,' Piglet protested.

Everyone could see that Piglet was afraid.

'The wind that blew these clouds is getting stronger and stronger! We should take cover,' insisted Eeyore.

There was a deep rumble.

'Well,' Pooh observed, 'there's a rumbly in my tummy. It must be time for a snack. You are all invited to my house!'

There was another rumble.

'That was the storm this time,' Eeyore said.

'Well, it looks as if I'm going to get wet again.'

Eyore had barely finished speaking when it started to rain. It not only started, but it continued raining, gently at first, then heavier.

'Could we go to my house instead?' asked Piglet, whose teeth were chattering. 'It's much closer!'

Pooh, Rabbit and Eeyore followed Piglet home. When they walked through the door, Piglet was nowhere to be found!

Suddenly, lightning struck, lighting the room. There was Piglet, under his bed!

'What are you doing under the bed, Piglet?' Pooh asked. 'Are you all right?'

Piglet didn't answer. A rumble of thunder answered instead.

'It sounds like the rumbly of my tummy,' Pooh decided. 'Do you think the sky is hungry?'

RUMBLE!

'I think it's almost as hungry as I am,' Pooh said whilst rubbing his round, empty tummy.

Soon, thanks to the wind, the clouds were blown further away, and the storm followed them.

'Oh! Oh! Oh!' shouted Tigger. 'There are puddles outside. Tiggers love to bounce over puddles. Let's go!'

'I'm not going outside,' protested Piglet.

'But the puddles are waiting to be jumped over by Piglet, too,' insisted Tigger.

'And my stomach needs me,' added Pooh. 'It needs some honey!'

'Are you all leaving?' Piglet asked, and jumped out from under his bed. 'Don't leave me alone with the thunder!'

When Piglet stepped outside, instead of a frightening, rainy wood, he saw a lovely Hundred-Acre Wood glistening from the freshly fallen raindrops. Frogs croaked happily, ducks quacked merrily and birds sang loudly.

'Look at all the puddles,' Piglet cried as he started to splash around.

'The best part of a storm is the splish-splashing once it's over,' Pooh exclaimed happily.

ut Winnie the Pooh was still very hungry and suggested that he and Piglet stop by his house for a bite to eat.

Eeyore was invited, too, but he had to check on his home. 'It's probably been destroyed,' he said, as he moped away.

So Piglet walked Pooh home. And once the friends had had their fill of honey, Pooh walked Piglet home.

That night, a light fog spread through the Hundred-Acre Wood. When the moon rose, its light shone like a halo through the mist.

Owl spread his wings. 'It looks like a fine and sunny day for tomorrow,' he said.

'Really?' Piglet said, looking a little disappointed. 'I was hoping it would rain again.'